The Pied Piper
and the
Wrong Song

Written by Laura North

Illustrated by Scoular Anderson

Crabtree Publishing Company

www.crabtreebooks.com

Crabtree Publishing Company
www.crabtreebooks.com
1-800-387-7650

616 Welland Ave.   PMB 59051, 350 Fifth Ave.
St. Catharines, ON   59th Floor,
L2M 5V6   New York, NY 10118

Published by Crabtree Publishing in 2015

To Dylan — L.N.

Series editor: Melanie Palmer
Editor: Kathy Middleton
Proofreader: Shannon Welbourn
Notes to adults: Reagan Miller
Series advisor: Catherine Glavina
Series designer: Peter Scoulding
Production coordinator and
   Prepress technician: Margaret Amy Salter
Print coordinator: Katherine Berti

First published in 2013
by Franklin Watts
(A division of Hachette
Children's Books)

Printed in
Canada/022015/IH20141209

Library and Archives Canada
Cataloguing in Publication

North, Laura, author
      The Pied Piper and the wrong song / written
by Laura North ; illustrated by Scoular Anderson.

(Tadpoles: fairytale twists)
First published 2013 by Franklin Watts.
Issued in print and electronic formats.
ISBN 978-0-7787-1934-2 (bound).--
ISBN 978-0-7787-1960-1 (pbk.).--
ISBN 978-1-4271-7698-1 (pdf).--
ISBN 978-1-4271-7690-5 (html)

      I. Anderson, Scoular, illustrator II. Title. III.
Series: Tadpoles. Fairytale twists

PZ7.N815Pi 2015   j823'.92   C2014-907779-3
                                       C2014-907780-7

Library of Congress
Cataloging-in-Publication Data

CIP available at Library of Congress

This story is based on the traditional fairy tale,
The Pied Piper of Hamelin, but with a new twist.
Can you make up your own twist for the story?

In the town of Hamelin,
there were rats everywhere.

3

"The Pied Piper can help us,"
said the mayor.
"He plays a magic pipe that
makes the rats go away."

5

So the Pied Piper arrived in town.
"I will get rid of your rats!"
he promised.

Rid-a-Rat

"If you can do that," said the mayor, "I will give you ten bags of gold."

"No problem," said the Pied Piper.
He took out his magic pipe and
started to play.

The rats looked up at the Pied
Piper. Not one of them moved.

But one by one, all the cows in the town started to follow the Pied Piper's magic song.

"Oh no!" said the mayor.

"What are you doing?"

11

"I don't know what went wrong!"
said the Pied Piper. "Let me
try again."

This time all the pigs began to
follow the Pied Piper, dancing
in a line to his tune.

"Come back!" the mayor shouted to the pigs. "There goes all our bacon!"

"Oh dear," said the Pied Piper. "This doesn't usually happen."

"Let me try again," said the Pied Piper. He started to play.

All the farmers started to dance
along merrily, heading for the hills.

The farmers left their gates open, and their farm animals escaped!

The goats were eating the flowers.

The pigs were sitting in armchairs.

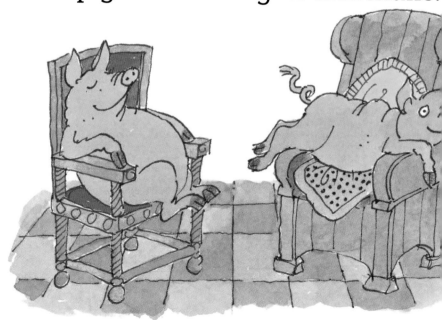

And the cows got into bed.

One clever boy named Peter had an idea. "Take these," he said, giving everyone earmuffs.

"You won't be able to hear anything that the Pied Piper plays."

The Pied Piper said, "I know I've got it right this time!"
He played his magic pipe.
But nobody moved at all.

24

No one heard a thing.

Not one rat, cow, pig, or farmer.

27

And the rats were still everywhere!
The mayor gave up. But the peopl
of the town paid the Pied Piper
—to go away!

29

Puzzle 1

Put these pictures in the correct order. Whic
event do you think is the most important?
Now try writing the story in your own word

Puzzle 2

1. I am an expert at scaring rats.

2. I have lots of bags of gold.

3. I have a magic pipe.

4. My town needs to get rid of rats.

5. I am busy running the town.

6. I don't live in Hamelin.

Choose the correct speech bubbles for each character. Can you think of any others? Turn the page to find the answers for both pages.

Notes for adults

TADPOLES: Fairytale Twists are engaging, imaginative stories designed for early fluent readers. The books may also be used for read-alouds or shared reading with young children

TADPOLES: Fairytale Twists are humorous stories with a unique twist on traditional fairy tales. Each story can be compared to the original fairy tale, or appreciated on its own. Fairy tales are a key type of literary text found in the Common Core State Standards.

THE FOLLOWING PROMPTS BEFORE, DURING, AND AFTER READING SUPPORT LITERACY SKILL DEVELOPMENT AND CAN ENRICH SHARED READING EXPERIENCES:

1. **Before Reading**: Do a picture walk through the book, previewing the illustrations. Ask the reader to predict what will happen in the story. For example, ask the reader what he or she thinks the twist in the story will be.

2. **During Reading**: Encourage the reader to use context clues and illustrations to determine the meaning of unknown words or phrases.

3. **During Reading**: Have the reader stop midway through the book to revisit his or her predictions. Does the reader wish to change his or her predictions based on what they have read so far?

4. **During and After Reading**: Encourage the reader to make different connections:
   Text-to-Text: How is this story similar to/different from other stories you have read?
   Text-to-World: How are events in this story similar to/different from things that happen in the real world?
   Text-to-Self: Does a character or event in this story remind you of anything in your own life?

5. **After Reading**: Encourage the child to reread the story and to retell it using his or her own words. Invite the child to use the illustrations as a guide.

HERE ARE OTHER TITLES FROM TADPOLES: FAIRYTALE TWISTS FOR YOU TO ENJOY:

Cinderella's Big Foot	978-0-7787-0440-9 RLB	978-0-7787-0448-5 PB
Hansel and Gretel and the Green Witch	978-0-7787-1928-1 RLB	978-0-7787-1954-0 PB
Jack and the Bean Pie	978-0-7787-0441-6 RLB	978-0-7787-0449-2 PB
Little Bad Riding Hood	978-0-7787-0442-3 RLB	978-0-7787-0450-8 PB
Princess Frog	978-0-7787-0443-0 RLB	978-0-7787-0452-2 PB
Rapunzel and the Prince of Pop	978-0-7787-1929-8 RLB	978-0-7787-1955-7 PB
Rumpled Stilton Skin	978-0-7787-1930-4 RLB	978-0-7787-1956-4 PB
Sleeping Beauty—100 Years Later	978-0-7787-0444-7 RLB	978-0-7787-0479-9 PB
Snow White Sees the Light	978-0-7787-1931-1 RLB	978-0-7787-1957-1 PB
The Elves and the Trendy Shoes	978-0-7787-1932-8 RLB	978-0-7787-1958-8 PB
The Emperor's New Uniform	978-0-7787-1933-5 RLB	978-0-7787-1959-5 PB
The Lovely Duckling	978-0-7787-0445-4 RLB	978-0-7787-0480-5 PB
The Princess and the Frozen Peas	978-0-7787-0446-1 RLB	978-0-7787-0481-2 PB
The Three Frilly Goats Fluff	978-0-7787-1935-9 RLB	978-0-7787-1961-8 PB
The Three Little Pigs and the New Neighbor	978-0-7787-0447-8 RLB	978-0-7787-0482-9 PB

VISIT WWW.CRABTREEBOOKS.COM FOR OTHER CRABTREE BOOKS.

Answers
Puzzle 1
The correct order is: 1c, 2e, 3f, 4b, 5a, 6d
Puzzle 2
The Pied Piper: 1, 3, 6
The mayor: 2, 4, 5